TrICK OR TREAT, OLD ARMADILLO

LARRY DANE BRIMNER

TRICK OR TREAT, OLD ARMADILLO

ILLUSTRATED BY
DOMINIC CATALANO

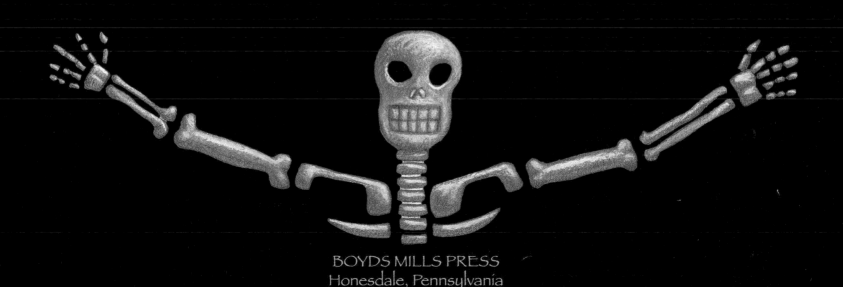

BOYDS MILLS PRESS
Honesdale, Pennsylvania

To children everywhere who love a good trick and a treat
—L.D.B.

For Oksana, the true love of my life—trick or treat!
—D.C.

Text copyright © 2010 by Larry Dane Brimner
Illustrations copyright © 2010 by Dominic Catalano
All rights reserved

Boyds Mills Press, Inc.
815 Church Street
Honesdale, Pennsylvania 18431
Printed in the United States of America

Library of Congress Cataloging-in-Publication Data

Brimner, Larry Dane.
 Trick or treat, Old Armadillo / Larry Dane Brimner ; illustrated by Dominic Catalano. — 1st ed.
   p. cm.
 Summary: On Halloween, Old Armadillo sits inside his little house waiting for his friends
to come trick-or-treating.
 ISBN 978-1-59078-758-8 (hardcover : alk. paper)
[1. Halloween—Fiction. 2. Animals—Southwest, New—Fiction. 3. Southwest, New—Fiction.]
I. Catalano, Dominic, ill. II. Title.
 PZ7.B767Ts 2010   [E]—dc22   2010004342

First edition
The text of this book is set in 14-point Palatino.
The illustrations are done in pastels.

10 9 8 7 6 5 4 3 2 1

Glossary

casita (cuh-SEE-tuh) —a small house
dulces (DOOL-ces) —sweets
esqueleto (es-kay-LAY-to) —skeleton
queremos (kair-A-mos) —we want

quiero (ke-AIR-o) —I want
sí (see) —yes
también (tom-be-EN) —too, also

Note: Halloween isn't a tradition in Mexico, because it occurs
at the same time as *Los Días de los Muertos* (The Days of the Dead)
celebrations. But in those places where it is celebrated, instead of
saying "Trick or treat," children call "¡*Queremos* Halloween!" on
Halloween night.

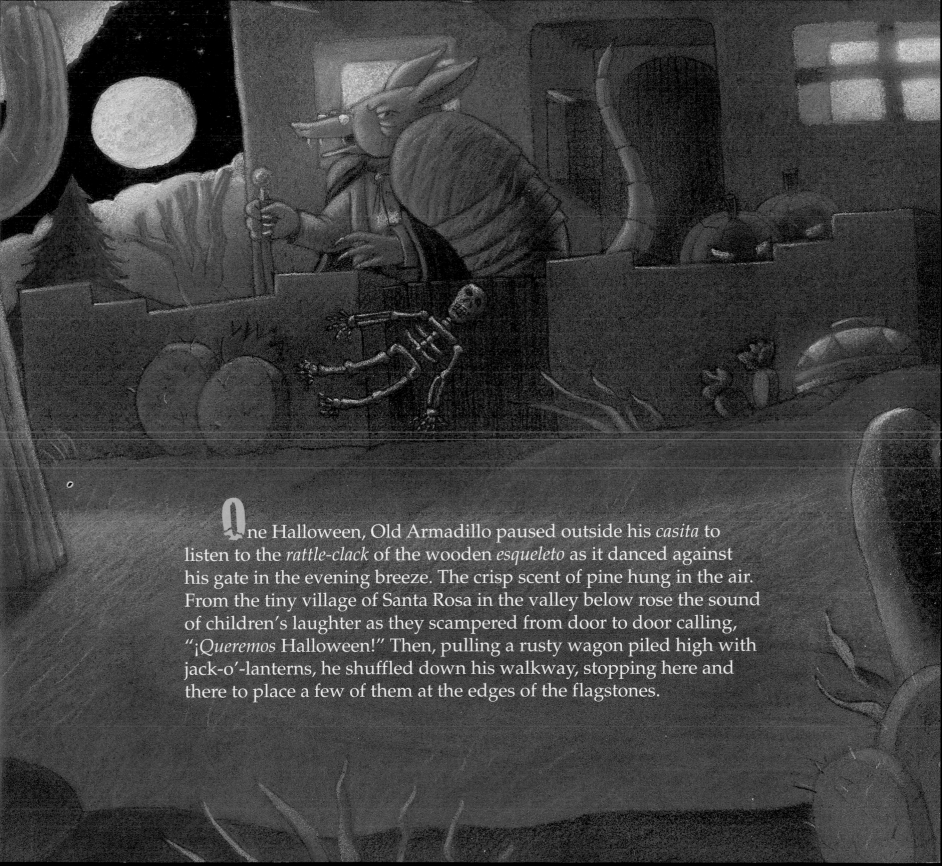

One Halloween, Old Armadillo paused outside his *casita* to
listen to the *rattle-clack* of the wooden *esqueleto* as it danced against
his gate in the evening breeze. The crisp scent of pine hung in the air.
From the tiny village of Santa Rosa in the valley below rose the sound
of children's laughter as they scampered from door to door calling,
"¡*Queremos* Halloween!" Then, pulling a rusty wagon piled high with
jack-o'-lanterns, he shuffled down his walkway, stopping here and
there to place a few of them at the edges of the flagstones.

Looking back at his walkway, Old Armadillo checked his timepiece one more time. "*Sí,*" he said to no one but the harvest moon. "*Quiero* Halloween, *también.*" He nodded. "I want Halloween, too." Then he hurried back inside, cozied up by the fire with a mug of hot cocoa, and waited for ghosts and ghouls, fair princesses and pirates to knock at his door.

Old Armadillo waited and sighed. He sighed and waited. Then he began to pace, stopping to peek out the window into the dusky night.

Nobody was there.

Outside . . .

A headless mummy wibbled and wobbled along the path and into Old Armadillo's garden. It was Roadrunner, and he chuckled to himself as he followed his shadow to the base of a giant saguaro. There he hid beneath the outstretched arms of the ancient cactus.

Inside . . . Old Armadillo paced.

Outside . . .

Hummph! Peccary tumbled into the garden. She pulled herself up and dusted off her shimmering gown. "Where are the others?" she asked herself.

"*Shhh,*" whispered Roadrunner, who toddled out from the shadow of the giant saguaro. "Over here."

He reached out to straighten Peccary's royal crown. Its jewels glittered like morning dew in the soft moonlight.

Inside . . . Old Armadillo listened. He peeked out the window. Then he returned to pacing.

Outside . . .

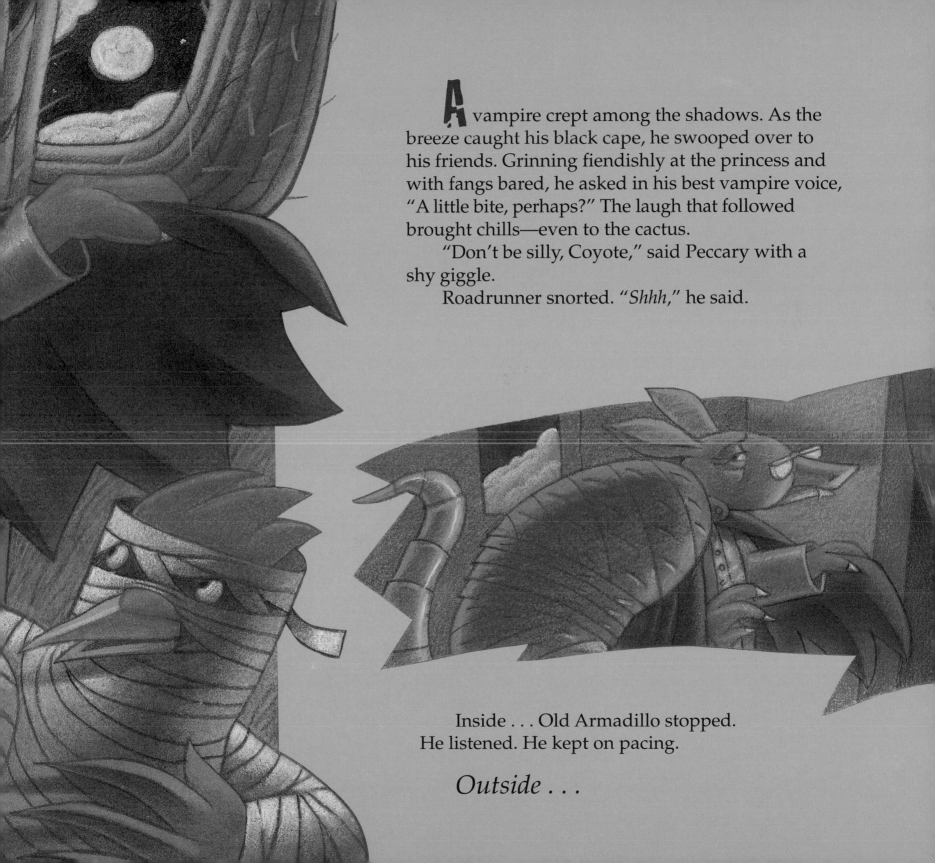

A vampire crept among the shadows. As the breeze caught his black cape, he swooped over to his friends. Grinning fiendishly at the princess and with fangs bared, he asked in his best vampire voice, "A little bite, perhaps?" The laugh that followed brought chills—even to the cactus.

"Don't be silly, Coyote," said Peccary with a shy giggle.

Roadrunner snorted. "*Shhh,*" he said.

Inside . . . Old Armadillo stopped.
He listened. He kept on pacing.

Outside . . .

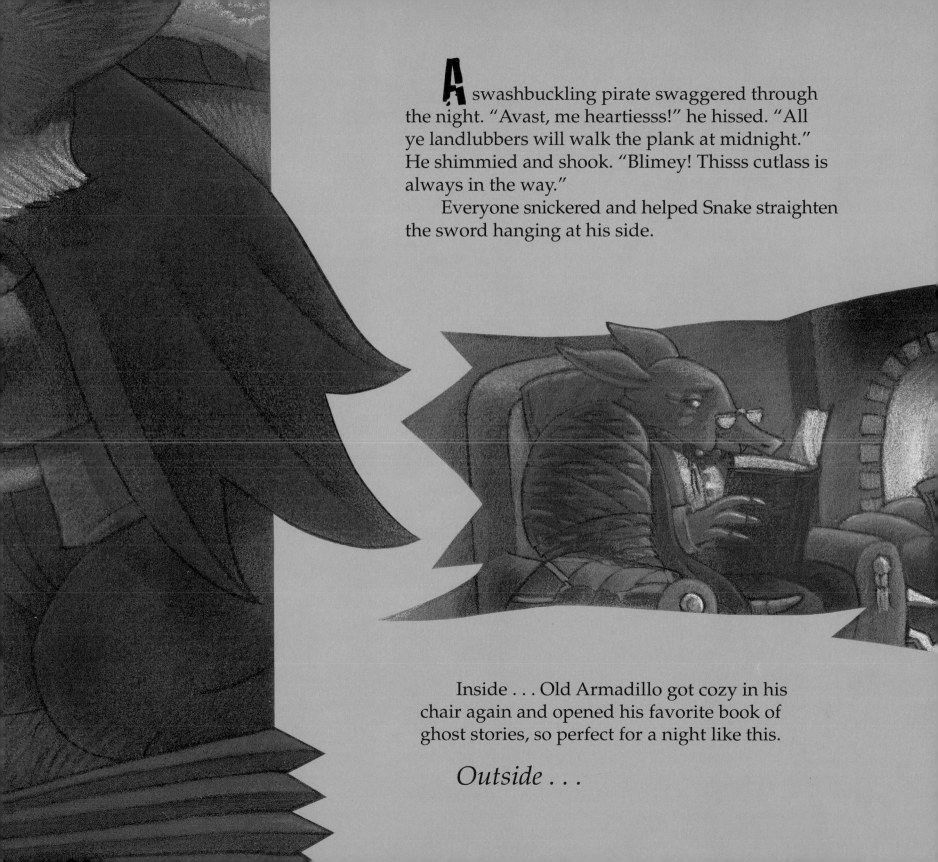

A swashbuckling pirate swaggered through the night. "Avast, me heartiesss!" he hissed. "All ye landlubbers will walk the plank at midnight." He shimmied and shook. "Blimey! Thisss cutlass is always in the way."

Everyone snickered and helped Snake straighten the sword hanging at his side.

Inside . . . Old Armadillo got cozy in his chair again and opened his favorite book of ghost stories, so perfect for a night like this.

Outside . . .

Voices chattered. "I hope we're not late," said Tortoise. The bolts on either side of his stitched-up head glinted in the silvery light.

"And I just hope Bear doesn't forget the treats," said Raccoon, peeking out from a flowing, ghostlike sheet.

"We're here," called the others quietly.

Inside . . . Old Armadillo took a sip of hot cocoa, turned the page, and gave up a shiver. "Ooo!" he said, sounding uneasy, sounding scared.

Outside . . . something squeaked. Something padded in the soft, gauzy light.

"**I** heard that, pardner," said Bear to Tortoise and Raccoon. Behind him, the masked cowboy pulled a squeaky wooden wagon filled with gold-colored bags.

"Treasure!" exclaimed Snake.

"Treats," said Bear. Then he turned his attention back to Tortoise and Raccoon. "I forget many things, but not old friends. And *not* treats."

"I'm sure they're his favorite," said Peccary kindly.

Inside . . . Old Armadillo turned a page and peeked through his fingers to read it. "Ooooo!" he uttered, even more fearfully than before.

Outside . . . figures slipped among shadows as the last sounds of laughter in the valley below began to fade and children hastened home to their *casitas* with their bounties of *dulces*.

Inside . . . Old Armadillo closed his book and listened.

Outside . . . feet scuffed upon flagstones.

Inside . . . Old Armadillo slowly pulled a blanket over his head.

Outside . . .

A paw pounded thrice against the door.

Inside . . . Old Armadillo shifted and squirmed beneath the blanket.

Outside . . . a chilling voice called,

"IT IS TIME!"

Inside . . . under the blanket, Old Armadillo grew as still and silent as stone.

Outside . . . the door handle rattled. The hinges squeaked. The door slowly swung open and feet tiptoed.

Inside . . . a mounded blanket slowly, silently rose from Old Armadillo's favorite chair to greet the intruders, and eyes grew to twice their size.

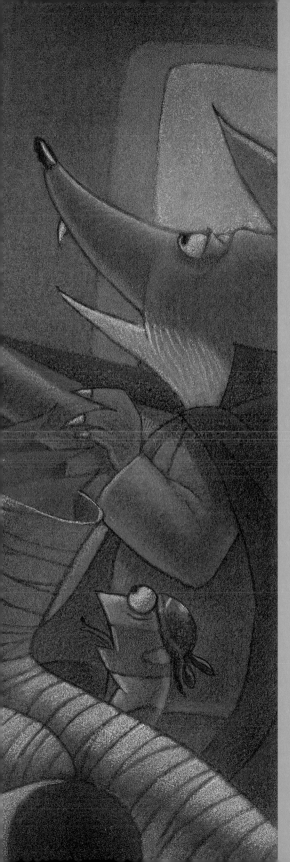

"¿*Queremos* Halloween?" gulped the frightened group.

Suddenly, Old Armadillo flung the blanket aside. "¡*Quiero* Halloween!" he called, his voice thundering out from a jack-o'-lantern. Then, looking at the intruders, he nearly doubled over. "My old friends," he said, laughing. "Trick? Or treat?"

"Treat," said Bear, breathing again. He gave
Old Armadillo one of the golden bags.

Old Armadillo peeked inside. "Bear, you remembered
that these are my favorite."

Dipping his head, Bear touched the brim of his
cowboy hat. Then he gave the others their treats, too.

"Trick or treat, Old Armadillo," said his friends, and one by one they took a turn at trying to scare each other with spooky stories that they told in front of the crackling fire.

As Peccary finished her tale, Old Armadillo listened
to each and every gulp and gasp and shivery shiver. Then
he popped another lemon drop into his mouth. He thought,
Halloween! So deliciously frightful!

"Happy Halloween, everyone!"